KONDO & KEZUMI

visit
GIANT ISLAND

Written by David Goodner
Illustrated by Andrea Tsurumi

LITTLE, BROWN AND COMPANY
New York   Boston

About This Book

The illustrations for this book were drawn in pencil and rendered digitally.
The text was set in Bembo MT Pro, and the display type is Inagur Pro.

Little, Brown and Company
Hachette Book Group
1290 Avenue of the Americas, New York, NY 10104
Visit us at LBYR.com

First Edition: October 2020

Little, Brown and Company is a division of Hachette Book Group, Inc.
The Little, Brown name and logo are trademarks of Hachette Book Group, Inc.
The publisher is not responsible for websites (or their content)
that are not owned by the publisher.

Library of Congress Cataloging-in-Publication Data
Names: Goodner, David, author. • Tsurumi, Andrea, illustrator.
Title: Kondo & Kezumi visit Giant Island / by David Goodner; illustrations by Andrea Tsurumi.
Other titles: Kondo and Kezumi visit Giant Island
Description: First edition. • New York ; Boston : Little, Brown and Company, 2020.
Summary: After finding a map in a bottle, best friends Kondo and Kezumi build a boat and set
out to explore the islands near their own.
Identifiers: LCCN 2018027196 • ISBN 9781368025775 (hardcover)
Subjects: CYAC: Adventure and adventurers—Fiction. • Islands—Fiction.
Best friends—Fiction. • Friendship—Fiction. • Sea stories.
Classification: LCC PZ7.1.G6543 Kon 2019 • DDC [E]—dc23
LC record available at https://lccn.loc.gov/2018027196

ISBNs: 978-1-368-02577-5 (hardcover), 978-1-368-04605-3 (ebook)

Printed in the United States of America

WOR

10 9 8 7 6 5 4 3 2 1

For Garrison and Ryan. Always explore. —D.G.

For Alexander, my partner in adventure. —A.T.

Something New

Kondo was big. Kezumi was little. They lived on an island with fruit trees and berry bushes and flitter-birds and fluffle-bunnies. The island had a crooked old tower and crooked old stones. It had wild rice and sparkle-flowers. And one day, the island had something new.

"What's that?" Kezumi asked.

"It might be dangerous," Kondo said.

Kezumi picked up the object. "It's a bottle," she said. "And there's something inside."

It was a rolled-up something. Kezumi opened the bottle, turned it upside down, and shook it.

Then she shook it again. The something was
stuck. She borrowed Kondo's stick and fished
it out.

The something was a drawing. Kezumi liked to
draw in the sand on the beach, but she had never
made a drawing like this one before.

"'We are not alone,'" Kezumi said.

"Of course not. We have each other," Kondo reminded her.

Kezumi held up the drawing for Kondo to see. "This is a map!"

Kondo and Kezumi looked closer. The map was full of islands. There were round islands. Lumpy islands. Square islands. One island looked like a curly snake. Another looked like a sea jumper.

"I wonder who else is out there," Kezumi said. "I wonder what else is out there." Kezumi was excited. "We should find out!"

Kondo was not excited. "We should pick berries. It will be dinnertime soon."

Kezumi helped Kondo pick berries. He could reach the high ones. She could reach the low ones.

Kondo picked a bumbleberry. It looked a lot like Bumpy Island. Kondo stopped to think. "Why?" he wondered.

"Why what?" Kezumi asked.

"Why should we find out?"

"I don't know," Kezumi said. She looked at the map again. Then she looked at the ocean.

II

Another New Thing

The next day, Kezumi started a new project.

"What are you doing?" Kondo asked.

"Building a boat," Kezumi said. "Help me move this log."

"Why do we need a boat?" Kondo asked.

"To follow the map," Kezumi said.

"What do you think we'll find?"

"I don't know. That's why we need a boat." Kezumi tried to move the log herself.

Kondo watched her. "What if there's nothing?"

"What if there's something?" Kezumi answered.

"What if it's scary?" Kondo asked.

"What if it's fun?" Kezumi answered. "We can't find the fun if we're afraid of the scary."

Kondo planted his feet in the ground. "What if I don't want to go?"

Kezumi jumped off the log. She looked up at Kondo. "Then I will be sad. And I will tell you all about my trip when I come home." She gave Kondo a hug.

Kondo moved the log for Kezumi. "What will we eat?" he asked.

"We'll bring fruit from the fruit trees," Kezumi said. "And berries from the berry bushes."

Kondo and Kezumi got to work
on the boat. It was hard.

They had to make it float.

Then they had to make it sail.

Then they had to make it turn.

Then they were ready.

III

Over the Sea

Kezumi and Kondo set off into the water.

"Where are we going?" Kondo asked.

"Let's sail around our island first," Kezumi said. "To practice."

Kondo was relieved. "Very practical."

They sailed close to shore. Then they sailed a little farther out. Then they came back to fix a leak.

After that, they sailed even farther out, until their island was small and far away.

Out at sea, the air smelled different, even though it was the same air. The sky seemed bigger, even though it was the same sky.

Kezumi looked ahead as she steered.

Kondo looked back as their
island got smaller and smaller.

Something jumped in the distance. "Look!" Kondo yelled.

Sea jumpers flew across the water and leaped over the waves.

Kezumi almost forgot to steer. "So pretty!"

"I've never seen them up close before," Kondo said. "Hi."

The sea jumpers swam closer and chittered hello. They followed Kondo and Kezumi, first on one side, then on the other. One jumped over the bow.

"Wow," Kondo said. "I wonder what else we might see."

"Oh, so much," Kezumi said. She pulled out the map. "Look at all these places."

Kezumi unfurled the sail and let the wind carry them home.

IV
The Voyage Begins

Kondo picked more fruit from the fruit trees. Kezumi picked more berries from the berry bushes. They were ready to sail again, longer and farther.

The first day at sea was exciting.

At night, Kezumi showed Kondo her favorite stars.

The second day was exciting, too.

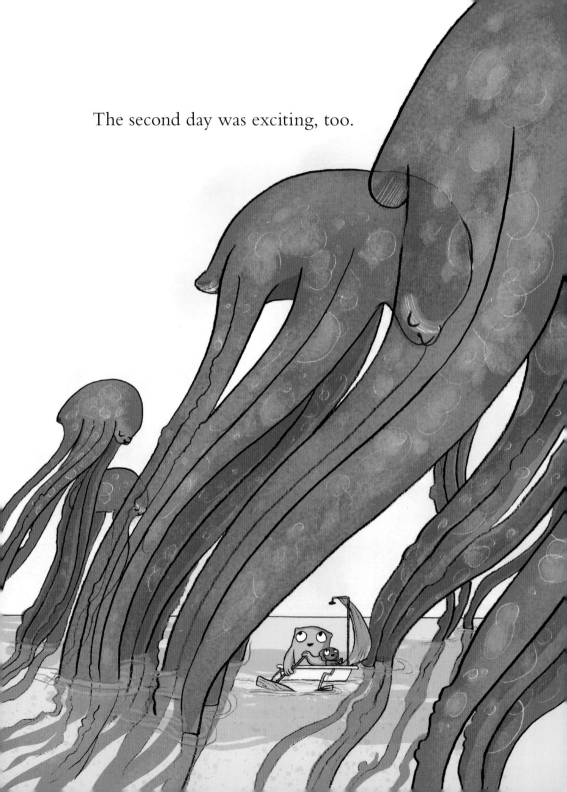

The third day was kind of exciting.

By the fifth day . . .

"This is boring," Kezumi said.

"There is a lot more ocean than I thought,"
Kondo agreed.

"Do you want to turn around?"

Kondo thought about it. "No," he finally said.
"I think there's land over there."

There was maybe a smudge of land. Or maybe it was a cloud. But either way, the current carried them toward it.

"What's that smell?" Kezumi asked.

Kondo smelled it, too. It was a
nose-wrinkly smell. A sharp smell. A
so-bad-it's-good smell.

"Is it . . . cheese?"

Kezumi looked ahead.
Kondo looked at the map.
Their boat wedged into
the shore.

It *was* cheese. An island of cheese!

There were grated-cheese beaches.

Cheese-cube mountains.

Cheese-leafed trees.

And even a cheese-gushing geyser. They found streams of milk and ponds of cream.

They made Parmesan sand castles and picked gourds of Gorgonzola.

"I like it here," Kondo said, munching on a cheddar log. "We could live here."

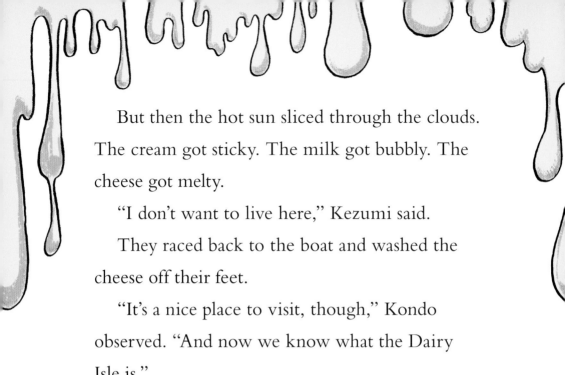

But then the hot sun sliced through the clouds. The cream got sticky. The milk got bubbly. The cheese got melty.

"I don't want to live here," Kezumi said.

They raced back to the boat and washed the cheese off their feet.

"It's a nice place to visit, though," Kondo observed. "And now we know what the Dairy Isle is."

He wrote a note on the map:

V
Beyond the Dairy Isle

Kondo and Kezumi sailed and sailed until the smell of Limburger was gone. Then they sailed a little farther just to be safe.

A plume of smoke caught Kezumi's eye. "Maybe that's another island," she said. "Maybe someone lives on it."

"Maybe someone is cooking dinner," Kondo said. He looked at the pile of cheese he had collected. "And maybe we can share."

They headed toward the smoke. It got thicker.
It got blacker. And it got smellier than cheese.

There was a cave on the island that looked like
a head. Fire shot out of its eyes. Lava dribbled
down its chin.

"That doesn't look like a friendly island,"
Kondo said.

It sure didn't. There were pointy plants and jagged black rocks.

"I think we found Fireskull Island," Kezumi said.

"I don't want to go to Fireskull Island," Kondo declared.

He wrote on the map:

"Do you want to go home now?" Kezumi asked.

"Kind of. I miss home," Kondo said.

Using the map, Kezumi showed Kondo where the Dairy Isle was . . .

and where Fireskull Island was . . .

and where their island had to be, since they'd sailed in a straight line.

"You've been really brave," she told him. "We can go back."

Really brave? Kondo liked being really brave. "We could go a little farther. There's a Fishy Island that I'd like to see."

"I'm not too sure about that one," Kezumi said. "But let's keep going."

VI

Things Do Not Go as Planned

The sun set, and the rain poured down on Kondo and Kezumi. A cold wind howled. Waves shook their boat up and down. All night, Kondo held the boat with one hand and Kezumi with the other.

In the morning, Kondo and Kezumi were wet and tired.

"That was scary," Kezumi said.

Kondo agreed. "I'm ready to go home."

"Me too." Kezumi pointed to the horizon. "Look!" The wind had blown them close to another island.

"Which one is that?" Kondo asked.

Kezumi was a little afraid to answer. "I don't know," she said.

"WHAT?!" Kondo said. "You don't know!"

"The storm blew us around." Kezumi held up a corner of the map. There were a lot of islands. "It could be one of these." Then she held up another corner of the map. "Or one of these."

"WE'RE LOST?!" Kondo cried.

"Please don't yell," Kezumi said.

"We're lost?" Kondo asked, quieter this time.

"Just a little lost," Kezumi said.

Kondo pouted. He had a very big pout. "I think we're ALL THE WAY lost!"

Kezumi sniffled.

That made Kondo feel bad.

"I'm sorry," Kezumi said. "This is my fault."

"No. It's not your fault," Kondo said. He realized something, too. Just because he was scared, he didn't have to stay scared. "You didn't make the storm. And you're smart. You'll figure out where we are."

Something Isn't Fishy

The new island looked a lot like their old island. There were flitter-birds and fluffle-bunnies. There were sparkle-flowers and big twisty trees. There was no crooked tower, though, and there were no crooked rocks, and the berry bushes had different-colored berries.

"Well, it doesn't look like a snake," Kezumi said. "And it doesn't smell like fish."

Kondo gazed at all the new fruits. "It's a good island, though."

Kezumi looked around. "Let's explore."

"Let's pick fruit first," Kondo said.

Kondo picked the high fruits. Kezumi picked the low ones. After the storm, after being lost, it was nice to do something normal.

Kondo tried to figure out how to open the new fruits.

Kezumi tried to figure out where they were. "It's not shaped like a big box. It doesn't feel lumpy. It's not very exciting, but I wouldn't call it Boring Island."

Kondo's fruit basket was almost full. Suddenly, the ground shook. Kezumi fell over. Kondo knocked over his basket.

"What was that?" Kondo asked. "Maybe this is Spooky Island."

"Or maybe this is Shaky Island," Kezumi said.

A thunderous rumble shook the trees.

"What was THAT?" Kondo asked. "This has to be Spooky Island!"

Kezumi studied the map. "If it were Spooky Island, we'd be able to smell Spaghetti Island."

"ZNORT," came a snort. "GRUMM," came a groan. Whatever snorted and groaned, it was something loud. Something big. Then the something asked,

WHO'S THERE?

"WHAT WAS THAT?!" Kondo cried. "Is there a Talky Island?"

The earth quaked. Flitter-birds squawked and flew away. Fluffle-bunnies ran for cover.

Kezumi held on to Kondo's leg. "Someone is in the mountain."

The mountain leaned down.

"I think the someone IS the mountain,"
Kondo said.
The mountain opened
one giant eye, then another.

"Maybe we should go," Kezumi said.

"Maybe we should put the fruit

back," Kondo said.

VIII

Albert

Kezumi looked up, way up. "This must be . . . Giant Island."

"GIANT ISLAND?" The mountain laughed. "MY NAME IS ALBERT."

"You are very big, Albert," Kezumi said. "My name is Kezumi. This is Kondo."

"I used to think I was very big," Kondo said.

"HOW DID YOU GET HERE?" Albert asked.

"We came in our boat," Kondo said.

"From another island," Kezumi added.

"I'VE NEVER BEEN TO ANOTHER
ISLAND," Albert said.

"Why not?" Kezumi asked.

"WHAT IF I DIDN'T LIKE THE FOOD?
WHAT IF I DIDN'T LIKE THE PEOPLE?
WHAT IF THE PEOPLE DIDN'T LIKE ME?"

"Are you lonely?" Kezumi asked. She wanted to give Albert a hug, but her hugs were barely big enough for Kondo.

Kondo understood. "Traveling is scary—and exciting."

"I WOULD LOVE TO HEAR ABOUT YOUR TRAVELS. WHERE DID YOU COME FROM? WHERE HAVE YOU BEEN?"

"We come from an island a lot like this one," Kezumi said.

"Except it doesn't move," Kondo added.

They told Albert about the
old tower and the flitter-birds
and the fluffle-bunnies.

While they ate dinner,
they told him about the
map in the bottle.

They told him about
building their boat.

They told him about the
chittering sea jumpers and the
Dairy Isle and Fireskull Island.

"THAT IS EXCITING," Albert said.

"Yup." Kezumi yawned.

"We should get some sleep," Kondo said.
"We have to leave with the morning tide."

"LEAVE?" Albert yelped. "Why would you
want to leave?" he whispered. Albert's whispers
were still pretty loud.

"We have to go home," Kondo said.

"But don't worry," Kezumi added. "We can have fun tonight."

"TONIGHT . . ." Albert mused. "YES. LET'S HAVE FUN."

It was their first ever sleepover. Of course, there wasn't much sleeping. Sleepovers aren't for sleeping. They're for playing games and telling stories.

Albert couldn't play
tag or hide-and-seek, but
he was good at I Spy.

And he could do tricks,
like blowing smoke rings with
the volcano on his forehead.

Albert didn't know many stories. He only had seagulls and sea jumpers to talk with, and all their stories were about fish.

Kezumi yawned a big yawn. Kondo yawned an even bigger yawn. "I think it's time for bed," he said.

"I'm not tired," Kezumi said. Then she yawned again.

"I am." Kondo closed his eyes and slept like a rock. (So did Kezumi.)

Albert did not sleep like a rock, even though he was mostly rock. Albert was too worried to sleep.

IX

A Surprise

Something was missing in the morning.

"Albert, where is our boat?" Kondo asked.

"OH," Albert said. "YES. THAT. IT BLEW AWAY."

"Oh no!" Kezumi cried. She looked up and down the beach. She looked far out to sea. The boat was nowhere to be seen. Kezumi sniffled.

"It'll be okay." Kondo hugged Kezumi.

She sniffled again. Losing the boat was worth two sniffles. Then she stood up straight. "You're right. It will be okay. We'll build a new boat. A better boat. With Albert to help, we can build the best boat!"

"I WILL HELP YOU BUILD A NEW BOAT. OR . . . I COULD HELP YOU BUILD A NEW HOUSE."

"Aww, that's nice," Kezumi said. "But we don't need a new house. A new boat will be fine."

"Hmm . . ." Kondo had a thought. "Albert, did our boat really blow away?"

"YES."

"But nothing else blew away?"

"UM . . ."

Kezumi gave Albert the stink-eye. Her eyes were small, just like the rest of her. But her glare was still very sharp.

"UM . . ." Albert said again. "IT DID BLOW AWAY . . . BECAUSE I BLEW IT AWAY."

"Albert! How could you?" Kezumi kicked Albert really hard.

Albert didn't feel anything. But he did start to cry. "I WANT YOU TO STAY," he blubbered. "I DON'T HAVE ANY OTHER FRIENDS, AND NOW YOU HATE ME!"

Giant tears fell down. Kondo and Kezumi used palm leaves for umbrellas.

Kezumi felt bad for kicking Albert. "We don't hate you, Albert." She patted his giant pinkie toe.

"We are mad, though," Kondo said. "Kezumi worked hard on that boat."

"I KNOW," Albert said. "I'M SORRY." He cried so many tears that Kondo and Kezumi had to climb up on his foot so they wouldn't be washed away.

Kondo leaned against Albert's ankle. "I know how lonely you feel. When I thought Kezumi was going to sail away without me, that was scarier than leaving my island."

"I WISH I WAS BRAVE LIKE YOU," Albert said.

"Oh, Albert." Kezumi's heart caught in her throat. "Come with us! You're so big you don't even need a boat."

"I CAN'T COME WITH YOU," Albert said. "I WISH I COULD, BUT THIS ISLAND IS ME. IF I LEFT, I WOULD BREAK THE TREES. AND WHAT WOULD HAPPEN TO THE ANIMALS?"

"That is a problem," Kondo said.

Kezumi agreed. "I'm sorry, Albert. I wish
I could fix it." Kezumi was good at fixing
problems, but she didn't know how to fix this one.

"We can't change Giant Island," Kondo said.
"But we can make it better."

"WHAT DO YOU MEAN?" Albert asked.

"What do you mean?" Kezumi also asked.

Kondo wasn't sure what he meant. "Well . . . we could visit."

"Yes!" Kezumi cheered. "We'll come back all the time! As long as you promise not to blow our boat away again."

Albert bit the corner of his lip and tried to be brave.

"I PROMISE!"

X

Making Things Better

Kezumi designed a new boat, bigger and better than the last one.

Albert knew where
the strongest wood
was for planks.

He knew where the
biggest leaves grew for sails.

And he knew where the
best vines were for ropes.

Kondo knew something, too—where to find
the best anchor.

"GOOD-BYE, FRIENDS!" Albert waved. He tried not to cry as he blew a puff of wind and set his friends off to sea.

"Do you want to go home?" Kezumi asked.

Kondo thought. "It was pretty scary. The storm, then losing the boat. But maybe we can go a little farther."

"Okay," Kezumi said.

"Let's stop by the Dairy Isle first, though," Kondo said. He made space for more cheese.

Kezumi added a note by Giant Island on the map:

XI

A Little Farther

Giant Island disappeared over the horizon, and the shadow of the boat stretched out before them.

"Are you excited?" Kondo asked.

"This part is a little boring," Kezumi admitted.

"Not always."

Up ahead, something sparkled in the water.

"It's the sea jumpers!" Kezumi cried. She raced to the prow to get a better look.

A pod of sea jumpers swam and danced across the waves. They frolicked in the ocean spray and splashed one another with their tails. As they got close to the boat, they chittered.

Kezumi waved. "Hey, are you going to visit Albert?"

One of the sea jumpers chirped and skittered alongside the boat.

"Do you think that means yes?" Kondo asked.

The sea jumper chittered some more, bobbing up and down.

"I think that means yes," Kezumi said.

Kondo waved to the sea jumpers. "Tell Albert we'll be back soon."

"With lots more stories," Kezumi added. "Because there are lots more islands."

THE END
(Not really)